D1109436

Daniel Plays Ball

adapted by Maggie Testa

based on the screenplay "Daniel Plays Ball" written by

Eva Steele-Saccio

poses and layouts by Jason Fruchter

Ready-to-Read

Simon Spotlight

New York   London   Toronto   Sydney   New Delhi

SIMON SPOTLIGHT
An imprint of Simon & Schuster Children's Publishing Division
1230 Avenue of the Americas, New York, New York 10020
© 2014 The Fred Rogers Company
SIMON SPOTLIGHT, READY-TO-READ, and colophon are registered trademarks of Simon & Schuster, Inc.
For information about special discounts for bulk purchases, please contact Simon & Schuster Special Sales at
1-866-506-1949 or business@simonandschuster.com.
The Simon & Schuster Speakers Bureau can bring authors to your live event. For more information or to book an
event contact the Simon & Schuster Speakers Bureau at 1-866-248-3049 or visit our
website at www.simonspeakers.com.
Manufactured in the United States of America 0714 LAK
First Edition
2 4 6 8 10 9 7 5 3 1
ISBN 978-1-4814-1709-9 (pbk)
ISBN 978-1-4814-1710-5 (hc)
ISBN 978-1-4814-1711-2 (eBook)

Whoever throws the ball,
picks an animal.

Then we all make its sound.

Miss Elaina picks a dog.

We all say . . .

Miss Elaina throws the ball
to Prince Wednesday.

He catches it.

Prince Wednesday picks a cow.

We all say . . .

Grr. I missed the ball.

"Keep trying. You will get better," says Prince Tuesday.

Prince Tuesday picks a duck.

We all say . . .

"Quack, quack, quack!"

Prince Tuesday throws
the ball to Miss Elaina.

She catches the ball.

Miss Elaina throws the ball to me.

Grr. I miss it again!

"Keep trying. You will get better," says Prince Tuesday.

I watch the ball.

Then I hug the ball.

"Nice catch,"
says Prince Tuesday.